To the Redfearn Boys,
Enjoy life's treats!

Gordon

8-11-11

A Farm Country
HALLOWEEN

by Gordon W. Fredrickson

illustrations by Michaelin Otis

ISBN 10: 1-59298-295-6
ISBN 13: 978-1-59298-295-0

Library of Congress Control Number: 2009933082
Printed in the United States of America
First Printing: 2009
13 12 11 10 09   5 4 3 2 1

Cover and interior design by Ryan Scheife, Mayfly Design

Beaver's Pond Press, Inc.
7104 Ohms Lane, Suite 101
Edina, MN 55439-2129
(952) 829-8818
www.BeaversPondPress.com

To order, visit www.BookHouseFulfillment.com
or call (800) 901-3480. Reseller discounts available.

To trick or treaters in farm country neighborhoods everywhere.

Photo courtesy of Evie (Cervenka) Mushitz

Halloween, 1950, and costumes were done.
We were ready to go trick or treating for fun!
We knew we'd be walking to visit each farm,
So we worked to make costumes both scary and warm.
We'd found an old sheet that would fit Maggie's size.
In the top we cut holes that lined up with her eyes.

Joey dressed like a tramp with his clothes patched and torn,
A mask on his face and his shoes curled and worn.
A pirate was I, with a sword made of wood,
A patch on one eye and a sack for a hood.
The sheath for my sword and the cape on my back
Had been cut from the side of an old flour sack.

Though very excited to be on our way,
We waited while Mother and Dad had their say.
"Be sure you are dressed for the weather," said Mother,
"And Joey and Mags, you must stay with your brother.

Regardless of reason, accept rides from none.
Be careful, polite, and, of course, have some fun."

When Mom finished speaking, Dad warningly said,
"By nine you had better be home and in bed.
When you visit these farms, play no tricks and no pranks.
Accept what is offered and then give your thanks.

Be good and don't follow what others might do.
Stay clear of Matt Schroedler's big dogs and his slough."

To the end of the driveway and then to the road
The Tramp and the Ghost and the Pirate each strode.
Then Maggie exclaimed, "On the moon overhead!
It's a witch's long broom!" and she shivered with dread.

"It's a cloud," I explained, "that is floating on by."
Then Joey yelled, "Wait! What's that *thing* in the sky?"
I replied, "It's a leaf that just fell to the ground."
Then we froze as we heard the most terrible sound!

Ee ee EE! Oo oo OH! Aa aa AH!" came a moan.
We huddled together, afraid to the bone.
We saw a dark figure along the steep bank,
Approaching us slowly. Our fearful hearts sank.

Then moonlight showed something that fast changed our mood.
We felt stupid to see 'twas our neighbor Jack Drude.
Three years older than I, so his laugh cut me deep,
Ashamed as I was at appearing so meek.

"You behaved like scared chickens," he mockingly said.
"You acted like you might just fall over dead!
You'll say you ain't frightened, but I know you are.
To prove that you ain't, you'll have to walk far.

You must walk our long driveway, near Schroedler's deep bog.
My pa says it's guarded by Schroedler's mean dogs.
You will come to our house, if you have any guts,
Unless you're afraid of Matt Schroedler's big mutts."

Jack laughed just before he escaped to the dark,
And we silently listened to distant dogs bark.
"Don't listen to Jack," my young sister said quickly.
"I know," I said loudly, "he's trying to trick me."

To the Droesers' we hurried all eager for sweets.
We knocked on the door and we yelled, "Trick or treats!"
The kitchen door opened and with a wide grin,
Mrs. Droeser said, "Golly, should we let them in?"

Mr. Droeser responded, "Let's do what they say,"
As he pointed to fudge that was stacked on a tray.
"If we give them the fudge they won't pull any caper."
We stared at the pieces all wrapped in wax paper.
"But first," said the Missus, "before you can eat,
You must tell us your names and remove the big sheet."

"Jim Carlson!" I stated, removing my patch.
"I'm Joey," he cried, "and this mask makes me scratch."
"I'm Maggie," she hollered, removing her sheet.
Then Joey asked softly, "So now can we eat?"

The Missus dropped pieces of fudge in our bags.
"I'm happy," she said, "that you're here, Joe and Mags,
And, Jimmy, you each look so handsome and tall.
I'll bet that your parents are proud of you all!

Since O'Kerans and Ryans were here long ago,
We're done for the night. You can take more fudge, Joe."

When we went to O'Kerans, it was much the same.
They gave us some cakes, and we each said our name.

When asked of our welfare, we quickly replied,
While trying to speak with respect and with pride.

At Ryan's big house, we were given to eat
Our very own box of a Cracker Jack treat.
Then we entered a room where we cordially sat
On a soft and long couch with our feet on the mat.

Mr. Ryan said, "Kids, no more candy you'll get,
But I'll give you a glimpse of our new TV set.
"There's a cow in the box!" Joe excitedly cried,
"But where is it hiding, behind or inside?"
Mr. Ryan laughed loudly and said, "Don't you know
It's the annual Godfrey big Farm Country Show!"

When we left, I told Maggie that I had to face
Jack's challenge to walk down the road to his place.
She said, "Going to Jack's isn't safe and, you know,
It's not one of the places Mom said we could go.
But he dared us to walk on the road through the slough,
If you think you must go, we are going with you."

On the sides of Drude's driveway the grass was so tall
That it moved in the breeze like a dark, living wall.
Low branches of willows, like hands reaching near,
Rustled in silence, increasing our fear.

"This fog makes it dark!" Mags exclaimed in alarm.
"And something is barking!" She reached for my arm,

As she nervously asked, "Are there ghosts in this bog?
That thing in the willow is not Schroedler's dog!"
I shuddered and uttered, "What *is* it I see?
A phantom is perched on a limb of the tree!"

As the phantom flew downward toward where we stood,
We started to run but our legs were like wood.

The phantom shrieked loudly, a terrible sound,
As I tripped on my sword, we all fell to the ground.

We braced for the worst as the phantom drew near
And made its attack. We were frozen in fear.

Would it bite? Would it scratch? Would it beat us quite dead?
As we huddled together, it passed over-head!

It hit a big tree with a staggering *whack!*
And the scream from the phantom sure sounded like Jack.
With a moan and a holler, Jack crawled to his feet,
As he tried to untangle himself from the sheet!

A rope had been fastened from willow to oak.
He'd hung from a pulley to pull his mean joke.

But we didn't dare laugh that his trick went afoul.
Charging toward us he let out a howl

That rattled the trees and shook up the night!
Frightened and angered, we braced for a fight.

Then out of the fog with a growl and a bark,
Huge creatures with fangs just emerged from the dark.

"The dogs!" Maggie screamed. "They're about to attack!"
We were ready to flee, but they ran straight for Jack!

We heard a girl yell, "Sic 'em, Shep! Get 'em, Mack!"
Mary Schroedler, our neighbor, had called the attack.
As the dogs followed Jack, Mary hollered, "You bully!
I made a mistake when I loaned you our pulley!"

Then she turned to say sweetly, "I'm glad you could make it.
I brought you all popcorn. I hope you will take it.

I popped enough corn for the neighbors to eat,
But nobody walked to our farm for a treat."

When Mary had left, my dear sister teased me,
"Jim has a girlfriend. It's easy to see!"
Ignoring her words, I said, "Dad was so right.
I should've stayed clear of all others tonight,

And we should've been home half an hour ago.
I'm sorry for leading you wrong, Mags and Joe."
"To our parents," asked Maggie, "how can we explain?"
"The truth," I said boldly, "will cause them less pain."

Joey looked worried, then said, "You were right
When you said I'd have fun trick or treating tonight.
I've a bag full of excellent sweets I can eat:
Cupcakes and fudge, and a Cracker Jack treat!"

And I'll never forget all the things that I've seen:
A big phantom, Jack's crash, and a cow on a screen!
It was scary but fun and although Jack was mean,
This night was a wonderful farm Halloween!"

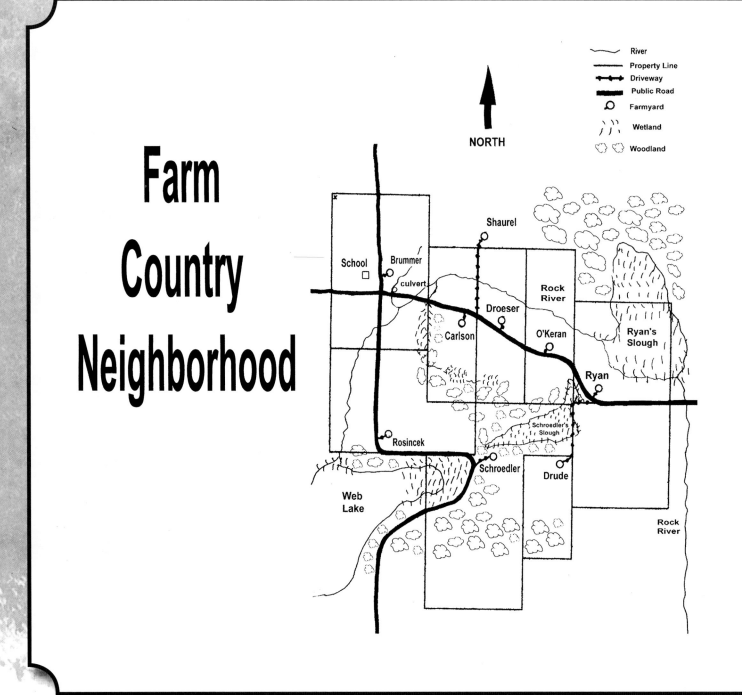

Farm
Country
Neighborhood

River
Property Line
Driveway
Public Road
Farmyard
Wetland
Woodland

NORTH

School
Brummer
culvert
Shaurel
Carlson
Droeser
Rock
River
O'Keran
Ryan's
Slough
Ryan
Rosincek
Schroedler's
Slough
Schroedler
Drude
Web
Lake
Rock
River

Trick-or-Treat Trek

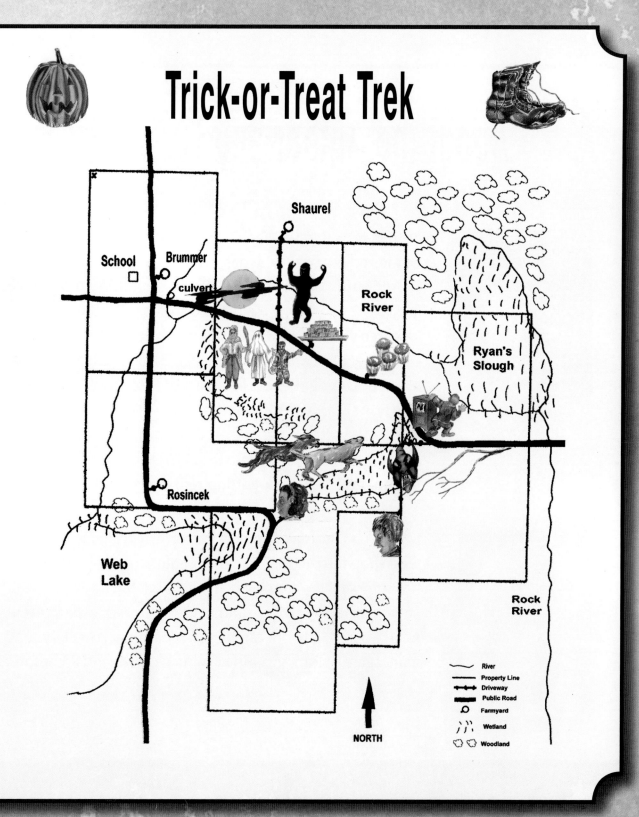

About the Author and Illustrator

Born in New Prague, Minnesota, Gordon W. Fredrickson was raised on a 120-acre dairy farm in hilly, rocky eastern Scott County, and like all the local farm children, he began farm work as a young child. Gordon served in the U. S. Army for three years, earned a Master of Education Degree at the University of Minnesota, and taught high school English for 16 years. During the first five years of teaching, he and his wife Nancy farmed 160 acres in western Minnesota where they raised cattle, hogs and grain. *A Farm Country Halloween* was inspired by events from his childhood. For more information, visit www.gordonfredrickson.com.

Michaelin Otis is a nationally known artist, illustrator, and workshop instructor. She has won numerous awards for her compelling watercolors and acrylics. Michaelin owned and operated her gallery and teaching studio, Avalon Arts, for 18 years. Her work can be seen at avalonartsgallery.com, manosgallery.com, shopuptownimages.com and Richeson School of Art and Gallery.